Grover's Guide to Good Manners

By Constance Allen
Illustrated by David Prebenna

A SESAME STREET/GOLDEN PRESS BOOK
Published by Western Publishing Company, Inc.,
in conjunction with Children's Television Workshop.

 Library of Congress Catalog Card Number: 91-73152
ISBN: 0-307-00127-X MCMXCIII

This educational book was created in cooperation with the Children's Television Workshop, producers of SESAME STREET. Children do not have to watch the television show to benefit from this book. Workshop revenues from this product will be used to help support CTW educational projects.

Hello, everybody! It is I, your furry pal Grover! Do you know what good manners are? Good manners are saying please and thank you and not putting your elbows on the table.

Would you like to learn about good manners? You would? Then please turn the page!

Thank you for turning the page!

Now, let us suppose that you have just met somebody new.

What should you say?

"How do you do?"

And now let us suppose that someone asks for a glass of milk.

What should he say?

"Please!"

Suppose that you have a new friend and you would like him to meet your mommy.

What do you say?

"Mommy, this is my new friend, Duane!"

And just suppose you have finished your dinner and would like to leave the table.

What is the polite way to ask?

"May I please be excused?"

Oh, dear! I have just accidentally bumped into someone! What should I say?

"I beg your pardon, sir!"

Oh, my goodness! Herry Monster just burped! He is so embarrassed!

What should he say?

"Excuse me!"

And what if someone gives you a glass of lemonade?

What should you say?

ICE-COLD
LEMONADE

"Thank you!"

"You're welcome!"

Suppose that you want to offer somebody your seat.

What should you say?

“Would you like to sit down?”

That is all we have time for today.
Thank you very much, everybody!
And please come again!